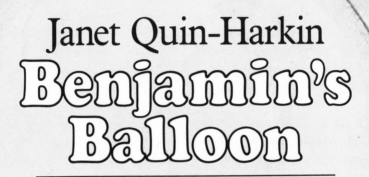

Janet Quin-Harkin

Benjamin's Balloon

pictures by
Robert Censoni

Parents' Magazine Press
New York

Text copyright © 1978 by Janet Quin-Harkin
Illustrations copyright © 1978 by Robert Censoni
All rights reserved
Printed in the United States of America
10 9 8 7 6 5 4 3 2 1

Library of Congress Cataloging in Publication Data

Quin-Harkin, Janet.   Benjamin's balloon.

SUMMARY: Benjamin's balloon carries him up
and away to adventure.
[1. Balloons—Fiction] I. Censoni, Robert.
II. Title. PZ7.Q419Bl   [E]   78-11225
ISBN 0-8193-0976-1   ISBN 0-8193-0977-X lib. bdg.

For Dominic,
who also will not stop
until he is ready.

One morning Benjamin found a balloon and started to blow it up.

He blew and blew.
The balloon got bigger and bigger.

"Stop blowing, Benjamin," said his sister.
"Your balloon has knocked over my dolls."
But Benjamin kept blowing.

"Stop blowing, Benjamin,"
said his mother.
"Your balloon has pushed
the clock into the fish tank."
But Benjamin kept blowing.

"Stop blowing, Benjamin!" shouted his father.
"You are squashing your grandmother."

So Benjamin went outside
and kept on blowing.

"Stop blowing, Benjamin,"
called the mailman.
"Your balloon knocked me off my bike."
But Benjamin walked on and kept blowing.

"Stop blowing," shouted a farmer.
"You are pushing over my cows."

But Benjamin kept on blowing
until he came to a big open field.
The balloon was now enormous.
"I wonder what would happen,"
said Benjamin, "if I let go
of this balloon?"
But, just then, a big wind blew.
It swept Benjamin and the balloon
up into the air.

"Darn," said Benjamin as he
held on tightly.
Over fields it lifted him.
Over towns and far away.

The balloon sailed over a city.
It sailed between skyscrapers.
People working on the ninety-ninth floor
stopped to watch Benjamin
speed past their windows.
Benjamin smiled at their surprised faces.
"This is fun after all,"
he said to himself.

The balloon was blown on and on,
toward high mountains.
It bounced off sharp snowy peaks
that sparkled like cake frosting.
But it didn't pop.

Then it sailed out over the ocean
and all sorts of sea birds
pecked at it.
But it didn't pop.

Benjamin and the balloon drifted over
a faraway island. The natives were afraid
and blew darts at the balloon.
But they missed.

Benjamin and the balloon were blown
to the North Pole. Eskimos hunting seals
threw spears at the balloon.
But they missed.

People in every town and village
all around the world ran out
of their houses to see Benjamin
sail past. Benjamin wanted to wave
but he didn't dare let go of the balloon.

Just when Benjamin began to feel
tired of holding on, the wind died down

and the balloon came to rest
near Benjamin's house.
Everyone came running to see
the gigantic balloon.
Benjamin held it high above his head
with one hand.

Then quickly, before another
wind could come, he let go.
The balloon went
WWHHHHHHEEEEEEEEE
EEEEEEEEEEEEEEEEEE
EEEEEEEEEEE

until there was no more air in it.
And Benjamin was content.

About the Author

Janet Quin-Harkin was born in Bath, England, and holds degrees from the Universities of Freiburg, Kiel and London. As a child, she dreamed of becoming a lion-tamer or an opera singer. Later, she went on to write plays for the BBC, manage a rock group, and, in 1976 she wrote her first children's book, *Peter Penny's Dance* which was judged one of the outstanding books of the year by *The New York Times*. Mrs. Quin-Harkin lives with her husband and four young children in Conroe, Texas. *Benjamin's Balloon* is her first book for Parents' Magazine Press.

About the Artist

Robert Censoni's cartoons have appeared in *The New Yorker, Saturday Review* and other magazines. The author-illustrator of *The Shopping Bag Lady* and *Cowgirl Kate,* Mr. Censoni was born and educated in Detroit. A well-known watercolorist, and a member of the American Watercolor Society, his work has been shown in major galleries throughout the country, and are in private collections. He lives in New York City and *Benjamin's Balloon* is the first book he has illustrated for Parents' Magazine Press.